tock. . .hummmmm. . .

The Goldfish

STORY AND PICTURES BY ELIZABETH SAYLES

HENRY HOLT AND COMPANY
NEW YORK

Henry Holt and Company, LLC, *Publishers since 1866*
115 West 18th Street, New York, New York 10011
www.henryholt.com

Henry Holt is a registered trademark of Henry Holt and Company, LLC

Distributed in Canada by H. B. Fenn and Company Ltd.

Library of Congress Cataloging-in-Publication Data
Sayles, Elizabeth.
The goldfish yawned / Elizabeth Sayles.—1st ed.
p. cm.
Summary: A sleeping child dreams of a magical sailboat voyage.
ISBN-13: 978-0-8050-7624-0 / ISBN-10: 0-8050-7624-7
[1. Dreams—Fiction. 2. Stories in rhyme.] I. Title.
PZ8.3.S2736Go 2005 [E]—dc22 2004022178

First Edition—2005
The artist used pastel on paper to create the illustrations in this book.
Printed in the United States of America on acid-free paper. ∞

1 3 5 7 9 10 8 6 4 2

This book is for you, Mom.

The goldfish yawned.

The firefly blinked.

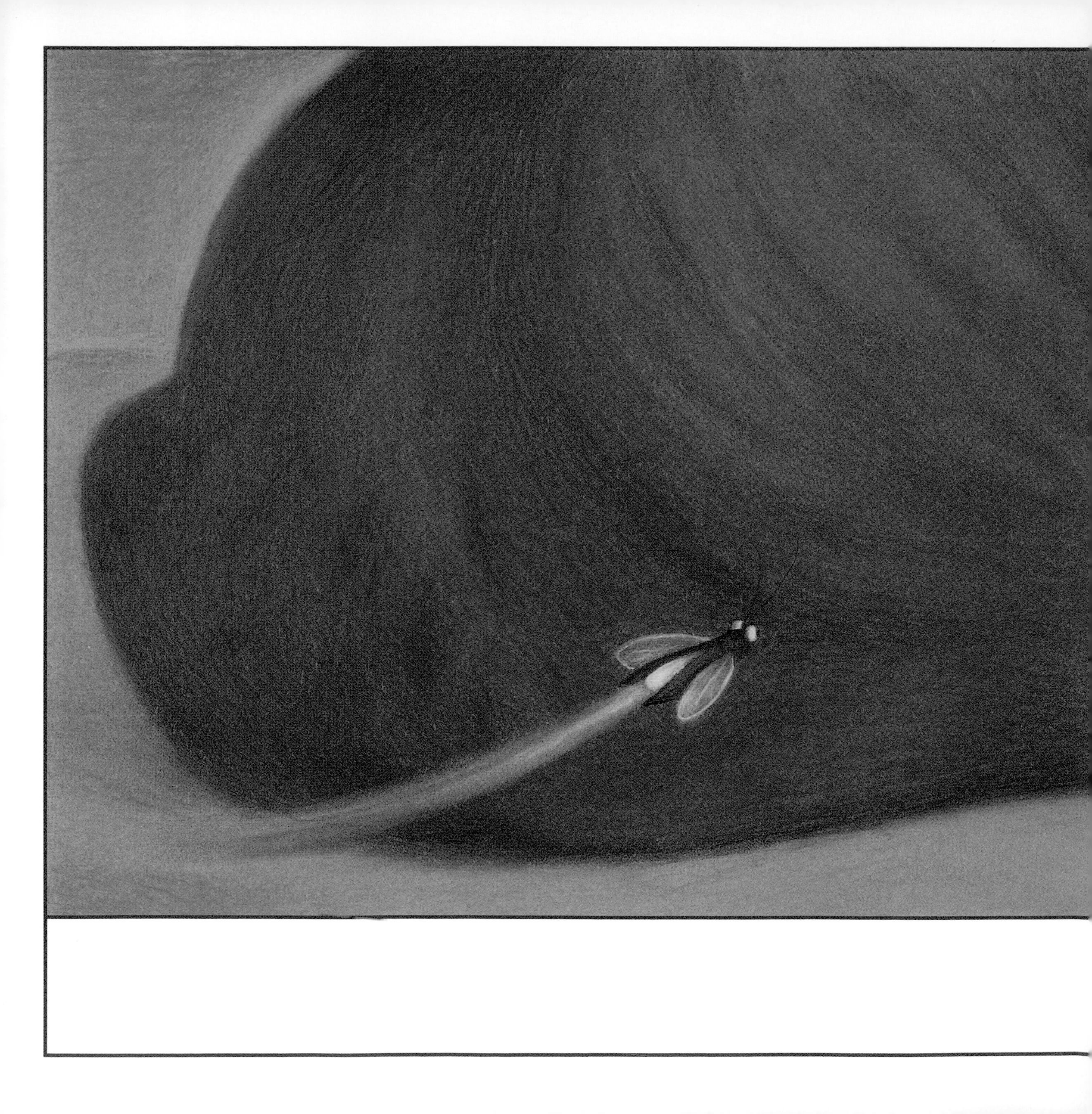

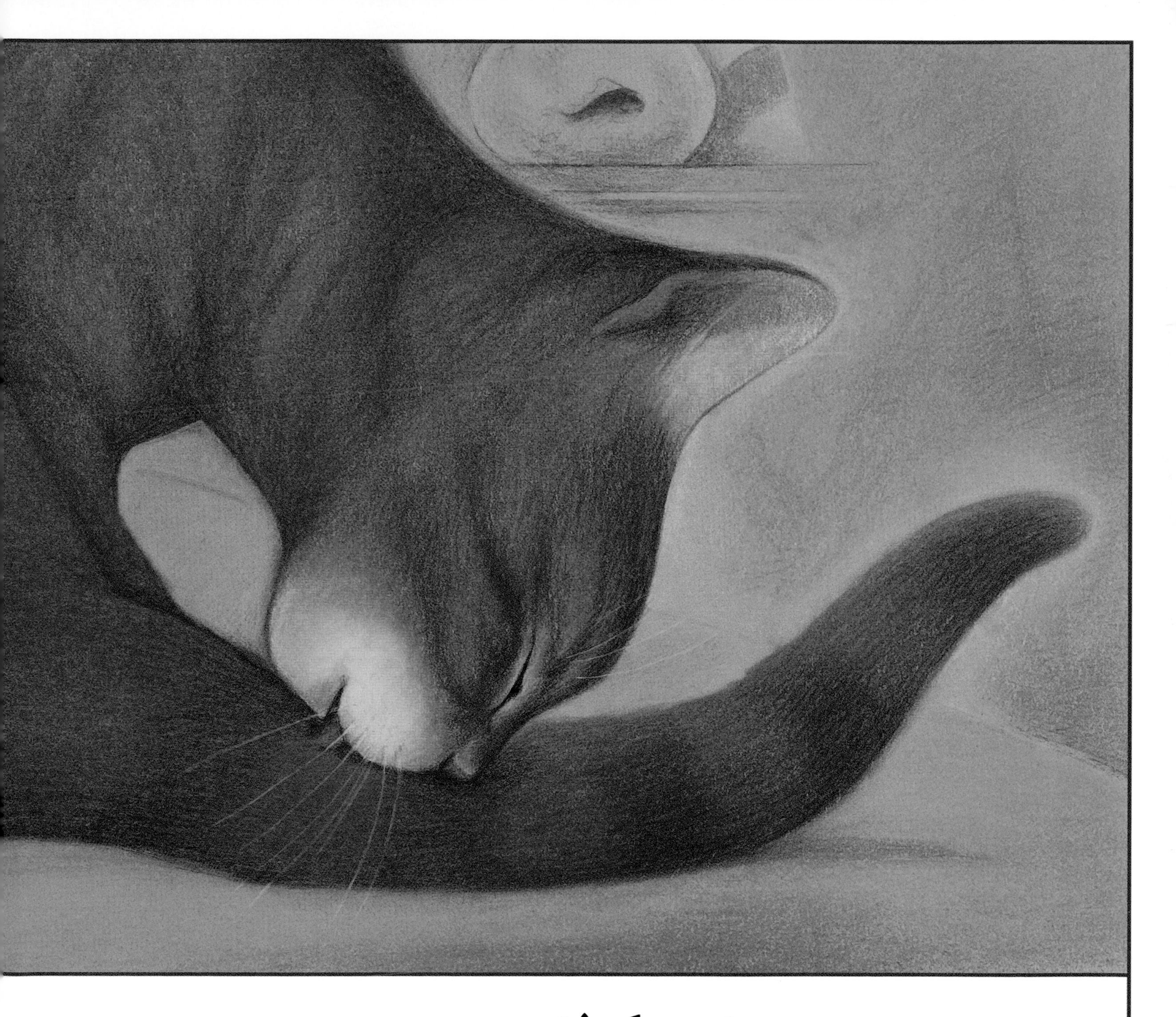

The yellow cat **licked** her tail.

The clock **tick-tocked**.

The night-light **hummed**.

On the rug, a ship **set sail**. . . .

The full moon rose.

An owl winked.

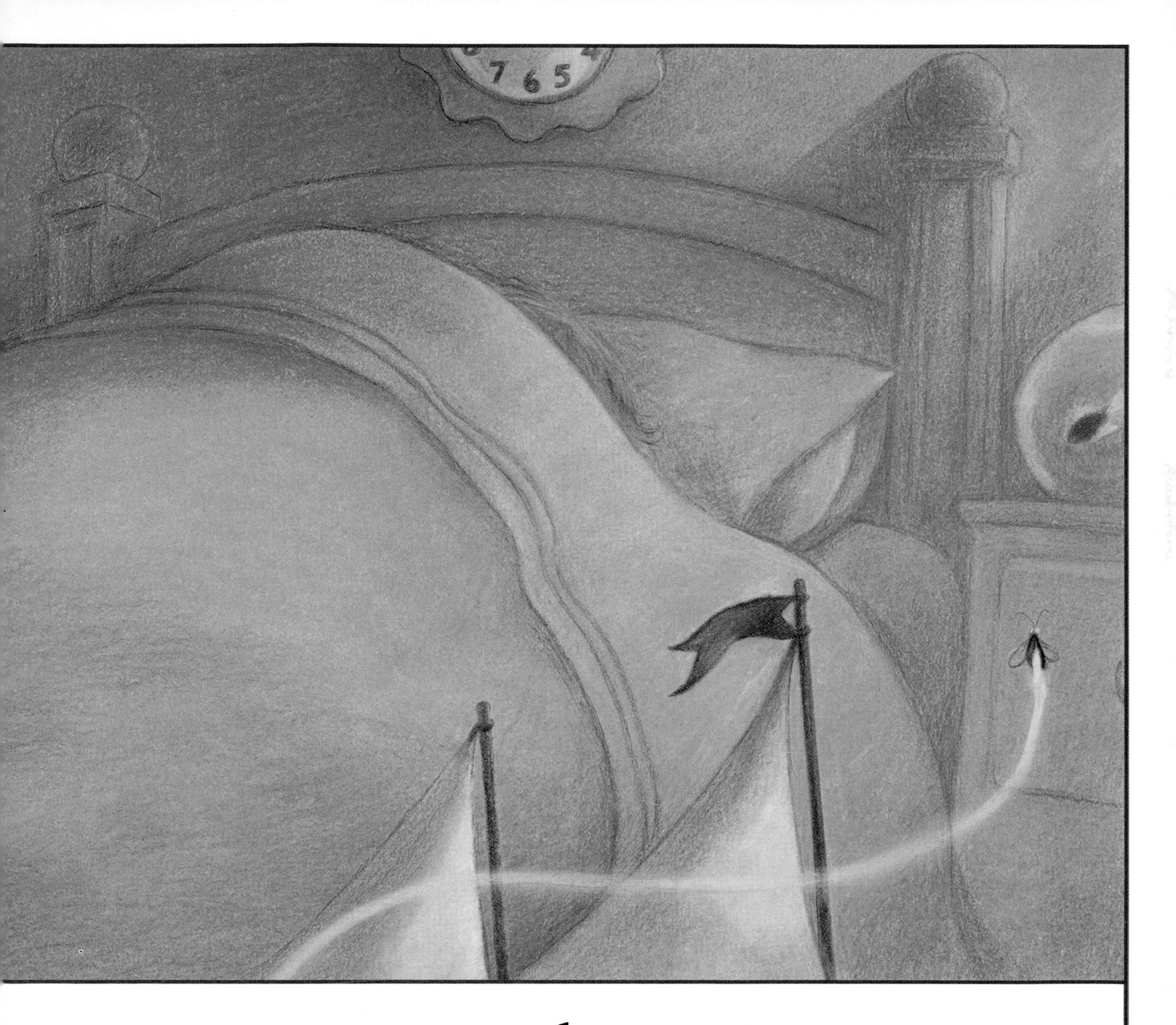

The yellow cat **cleaned** her feet.

The captain **steered** with a steady hand

past the sock and sneaker reef.

Yawn, blink,

tick-tock, hummmm.

The sails were filled with wind.

Raccoons tumbled.

An owl ho-o-o-oted.

Crickets began to sing!

The goldfish yawned.

The firefly blinked.

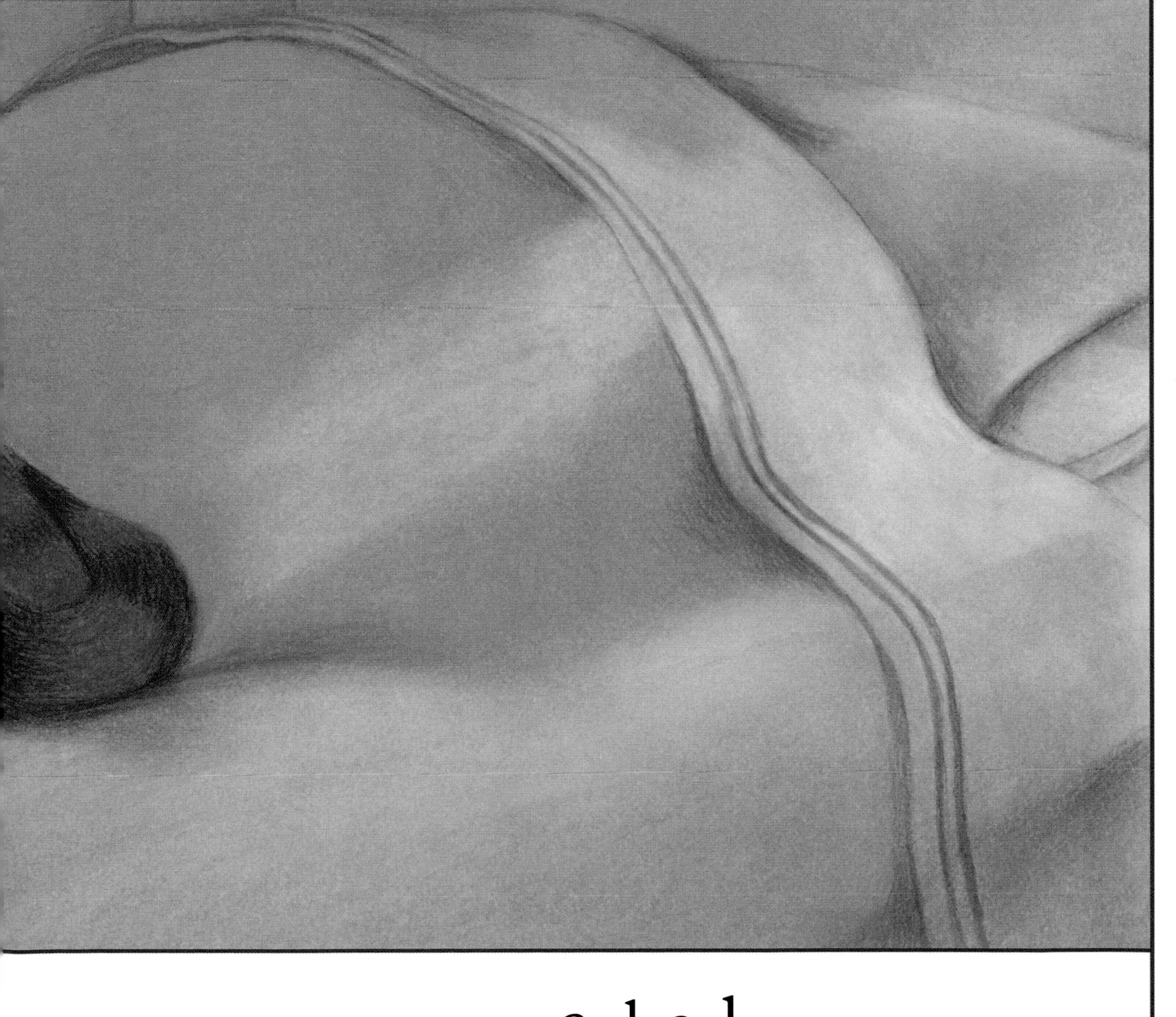

The yellow cat **washed** some more.

The ship sailed home

past the rising sun

to the rug on my bedroom floor.

Yawn

· · tick-

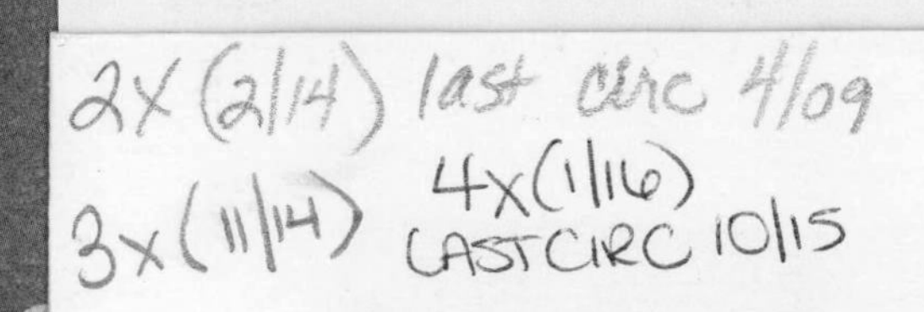